A Summer in the South

A Summer in the South

JAMES MARSHALL

A YEARLING BOOK

Published by
Dell Publishing Co., Inc.
1 Dag Hammarskjold Plaza
New York, New York 10017

Yearling ® TM 913705, Dell Publishing Co., Inc.

ISBN: 0-440-48105-8

Reprinted by arrangement with
Houghton Mifflin Company
Printed in the United States of America
First Yearling printing—November 1980
CW

For
Francelia Butler
and
Charity Chang

A Summer in the South

1

"The hotelkeeper should fire that goose," whispered Foster Pig to a small orange cat seated at the next table.

"She was hired at the last minute," said Mr. Paws, "and I'm sure the hotelkeeper could never find anyone to replace her. She does all the cooking, serves all the meals, and cleans all the rooms."

"And she makes a shocking mess of everything," said Foster Pig. "Just look at this disgraceful lunch. My potato chips are all soggy with pickle juice, and there are water spots on my drinking glass. I'm sure we're going to catch some dreadful goose disease. Have you ever taken a close look at her feathers? They're all covered with dirt and grease. Just yesterday I found three greasy goose feathers in my bed!

Not one, but three! Yes, I think I shall put in another complaint to the hotelkeeper," he said, raising his voice and turning in the direction of a colorful bird sitting beside the cash register and adding up a long column of numbers.

"I think the hotelkeeper is occupied with his accounts," said Mr. Paws.

"Humpf!" snorted Foster Pig. "Whoever heard of a turkey running a first-class hotel, anyway?"

Foster fell silent for a moment as a very beautiful chicken entered the dining room and sat down at a small table for one in the far corner.

Dabbing his lips with his napkin, Foster leaned closer to Mr. Paws. "She is quite attractive, but I have it on good authority that she was once a *circus chicken!*" He smiled a knowing smile and inspected his vest for any crumbs that might have fallen.

"I like the circus," said Mr. Paws.

A merry voice was heard from the kitchen.

"And furthermore," continued Foster in his complaining mood, "I don't approve of all that singing and dancing in the kitchen. It's a wonder that goose gets *any* of her chores done."

The kitchen doors swung open, and the goose appeared.

She was carrying dessert on a tray, and she was
singing a popular tune.

> You're my sweetie
> You're my pet
> You're the one
> I'm gonna get
> Sha la la la
> Doo dee dooo

"Silly goose," grumbled Foster Pig. "Doesn't have
a brain in her head." He dipped his spoon into his
pineapple Jell-o.

"Tasty, isn't it?" said Mr. Paws.

"It will do," said Foster Pig.

At that moment, two lively squirrel twins burst into

the dining room. They were young and foolish and
full of fun. "Surf's up!" they shouted.

4

Foster Pig dropped his spoon. "Outrageous! *Out-geous!* Imagine coming into a hotel dining room in bathing trunks!"

"They're only kids," said Mr. Paws.

The squirrel twins raced to their favorite table, with a view of the gulf. "Let's hurry up and eat, so we don't miss the big waves," said one to the other. "This is going to be a wonderful summer!"

2

After lunch it was siesta time, and all the guests, except the frisky squirrels, went to their rooms for an afternoon snooze.

"Now be sure to go far down the beach so you don't disturb the nappers," said the hotelkeeper to the squirrel twins.

The squirrels were gone in a flash, and a sleepy hush fell over the hotel. Very soon the peaceful sound of snoring could be heard everywhere. Someone was even snoring in the kitchen. Ceiling fans turned lazily in the warm afternoon air, and the clock in the lobby struck two. Outside, big blue green waves rolled onto the beach and tall palms cast their shadows across the closed blinds.

"I love my hotel," said the hotelkeeper to himself. Strolling on the wide verandah, he thought about the long summer season ahead. "I must make sure that my guests are comfortable and that they enjoy their stay."

Sitting down on the porch swing, he examined the list of guests. Almost everyone had arrived.

Foster Pig, of Foster Farms

"Now *there* is a cantankerous character, if there ever was one," thought the hotelkeeper. "So picky and hard to please. Foster started complaining the moment he arrived. And he is always so meticulous." Foster always carried a small feather duster wherever he went, just in case he found any dust.

Don Coyote, of Sneezing Springs

The hotelkeeper scratched his beak. Don Coyote seemed to be in delicate health. He spent most of the day in his room. "My health is just terrible," Don Coyote had said upon arrival. "If it's not my runny nose, it's my swollen toes. Or it's my lumbago, or my adenoids, or my tonsils, or my sinuses, or my hay fever. I also have quite a lot of nosebleeds. As you can see, I am really very sick. Just taking all my medicine is a full-time occupation. There are my blue pills with the yellow spots, there are my orange pills with the little red spots, and there are my lavender capsules. I also take lots and lots of cough medicine."

The Squirrel Twins, of Nutmeg Falls

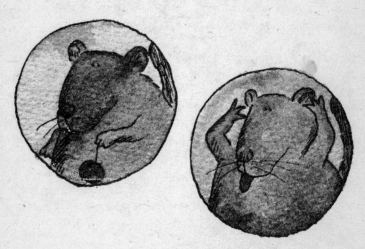

"I hope those kids don't make a lot of noise," thought the hotelkeeper. "My guests, especially Foster Pig and Don Coyote, won't appreciate a lot of racket."

"Such a beautiful lady," thought the hotelkeeper. "And always so serene, not at *all* like other chickens I have known."

Eleanor Owl, of Sherlock House

The hotelkeeper's eyes lighted up. Eleanor Owl was his prize guest. Who would have thought that such a renowned detective would be staying at *his* hotel? Eleanor Owl and her assistant, Mr. Paws, had come to the hotel for a well-deserved vacation. "Eleanor Owl has solved twenty-nine important cases," thought the hotelkeeper. "There was the famous Case of the Exploding Possum, and there was the Puzzle of the Talking Bubblegum. And of course there was the Disappearance of the One-Armed Octopus. And the Mystery of the Whistling Grandmother. And the apprehension of that master criminal, Boris Mongoose. And who could forget Alligator Jones? Yes, Eleanor Owl certainly adds luster to my guest list this summer."

The hotelkeeper looked at the next name on the list.

Mr. Paws, also of Sherlock House

"A nice gentleman," he thought. "Always cheerful and never complaining. If only some of the other guests could be like Mr. Paws."

There were only two names left:

"Such unusual names," thought the hotelkeeper. "I wonder who they could be and when they'll be arriving."

Very soon the hotelkeeper found himself nodding off, and he went inside to stretch out on the horsehair sofa in the lobby. It was not long before he too was snoring.

3

Bang! Sputter! Boom! Clatter! Sputter! Bang!!

A large station wagon, making a lot of noise, rolled up in the drive. Wild silly giggling was heard, and an enormous cloud of dust poured in the hotel windows. A horn honked three times.

In the kitchen the goose fell off her stool.

In the lobby the hotelkeeper snapped awake. "Guests are arriving!" he exclaimed, rubbing his scrawny wings together. "Maxine, Maxine!" he called out to the goose. "Rush outside and fetch the luggage!"

After some shaking and feather pulling, the goose was made to understand. Slowly she waddled across the lobby and pushed open the heavy screen door. But when she saw who was standing on the verandah, she let out a tremendous squawk and fainted away.

Some of the guests who had been awakened by the arrival came downstairs to investigate.

"Oh my goodness," gulped Mr. Paws.

Standing before them, her long hairy arms holding the stricken goose, was a large lady baboon.

The hotelkeeper cleared his throat and made a little bow. "Welcome to the hotel," he said in his best hotelkeeper's voice. "Please forgive that goose's atrocious manners."

Before the baboon lady could reply, the goose opened her eyes, let out an even louder squawk, and fainted away again.

"Just put her down on that horsehair sofa," said the hotelkeeper.

"I'm *so* sorry," said the lady. "I'm afraid I scared her."

"It's not important," said the hotelkeeper. "May I be of service?"

"I have a reservation for myself and my three companions," said the lady.

The hotelkeeper and the other guests looked out at the station wagon. Seated in the back were three more equally large lady baboons.

"Will you please sign the register?" said the hotelkeeper.

"Certainly," said the lady. And taking the pen she wrote in a large handwriting:

The Traveling String Quartet

"But of course," said the hotelkeeper. "How nice to have you with us. Allow me to assist you with your musical instruments."

"Oh no!" exclaimed the lady. "We'll bring those in ourselves."

"Musicians!" muttered Foster Pig under his breath. "There goes the last of my peaceful vacation!"

"Yes," said Don Coyote, "this will be terrible for my nerves." And he climbed back up the stairs to finish his siesta.

"Oh, I love good music," said Mr. Paws, following. The baboon ladies carried their instrument cases into the hotel and went to their room.

"Delightful, delightful," said the hotelkeeper to himself. "Things are beginning to pick up. Now if only that family, the Cooties, would arrive."

4

That evening, somewhere in the hotel behind a locked door, someone was writing a serious letter.

Dear Grandmother,

I have found a swell place to hide out until the heat is off. They will never think to look for me here. And I am acting my part really well. Even my own granny wouldn't recognize me with my new personality.

But I must be extra careful not to give myself away, especially with a famous detective like Eleanor Owl around. You never know when a clue might slip out.

Keep out of trouble.

Love,
You-Know-Who

5

"There is something suspicious about that string quartet," said Eleanor Owl to Mr. Paws the next afternoon.

"I know what you mean," said Paws. "They don't seem like musicians at all."

"Exactly," said Eleanor Owl, gazing out at the beach where the baboon ladies were wiggling their toes in the sand. "It's those hands. Most musicians have very beautiful hands, and those ladies do not. Clue Number One."

"And have you noticed that they haven't been practicing?" said Mr. Paws. "It's not like musicians not to practice."

"Clue Number Two," said Eleanor Owl. "But we shall find out everything in good time."

Mr. Paws looked concerned. "We must remember that we are here for a vacation. No investigating, just plenty of rest. Rest and relaxation, that's what Doctor Swan ordered."

"That old quack," said Eleanor Owl. "Investigating is very beneficial. Whenever I uncover suspicious activity, I feel tingly all over. Besides I just can't help myself."

Mr. Paws knew there would be no arguing with Eleanor Owl. "Let's go for a stroll in the dunes," he suggested.

"No," said Eleanor Owl, "let's mosey down the beach instead. Perhaps we can overhear bits of the baboons' conversation. I'm most curious about that foursome."

Eleanor Owl and Mr. Paws strolled ever so casually down the beach. They pretended to be looking for seashells.

"Here comes that detective," whispered one of the baboons. "Let's change the subject quick."

"Yes," said one of her friends, "talk about something musical."

"Oh *la*," said one of the ladies in a loud voice. "I was saying to Beethoven just the other day, 'Beethoven,' I said, 'your music is tops in my book.' "

Eleanor Owl raised an eyebrow and looked at Mr. Paws. "Clue Number Three," she whispered.

6

"What did you say!" gasped the hotelkeeper. "Big Ruby has hired musical entertainment?"

"That is correct," said Eleanor Owl. "I understand that Sloan the Singing Skunk will begin performing at Big Ruby's tomorrow night."

The hotelkeeper did not look happy. Big Ruby was his worst enemy. She ran the only other hotel on the beach, and she was always trying to lure away his customers. "That's just *like* Big Ruby," he said. "If some of my guests hear about Sloan, they may wish to change hotels. Musical entertainment can be very enticing."

"My advice," said Eleanor Owl, "would be to get some musical entertainment of your own. And I don't mean that goose who is always singing and dancing in the kitchen. Someone with talent and experience."

"You're absolutely right," agreed the hotelkeeper.

"Now *who* do we know who plays a musical instrument?" said Eleanor Owl.

The hotelkeeper paced back and forth. He was concentrating very hard.

"Who *do* we know who play musical instruments?" said Eleanor Owl.

"I've got it!" shouted the hotelkeeper. "We have musical talent right under our noses. What about the Traveling String Quartet?"

"What an original idea," said Eleanor Owl.

"But the ladies of the quartet are *professional* musicians," said the hotelkeeper. "I'm sure they would never consent to play for free."

"You could always offer them free desserts," suggested Eleanor Owl. "Free banana puddings, for example."

The hotelkeeper thought that was a splendid idea, and he immediately approached the baboons, who were sipping iced tea on the verandah and whispering among themselves.

"Oh no, we couldn't possibly play," said one of the ladies.

"My, my, ladies," said Eleanor Owl, stepping from behind a potted palm. "One would think you weren't *interested* in music. No musician I know would *ever* pass up an opportunity to make music."

"Er," mumbled one of the ladies.

"Uh," said another.

21

"You don't understand," said the third lady baboon.

"I think I understand very well," replied Eleanor Owl.

"It's because we forgot to bring our music!" the fourth lady suddenly announced.

"Yes, that's it," said the others. "We forgot to bring our music. We can't possibly be expected to play without our music."

"Oh," said Eleanor Owl. "How unfortunate."

7

That night, after all the guests had gone to bed, there was a terrific commotion.

"Help! Help!" screamed Don Coyote. "Help! This place is haunted!"

The hotelkeeper in his pajamas rushed into Don Coyote's room. Don Coyote was hiding under the bed. His teeth were chattering.

"What seems to be the trouble?" said the hotelkeeper in calm, reasonable tones. At hotelkeepers' school, he had been taught never to get excited.

"I have just seen a ghost!" cried Don Coyote. "This very minute, in the hall! It nearly scared me to death! As if I wasn't sick enough already!"

"Perhaps it was only your imagination," said the hotelkeeper, who didn't believe in ghosts.

"Why do people always say that?" cried Don Coyote. "I *have* just seen a ghost!"

"What did it look like?" asked the hotelkeeper.

"What do all ghosts look like?" said Don Coyote. "It was all white and scary."

"Then perhaps it was only Eleanor Owl in her nightie," said the hotelkeeper. "She does not sleep much at night, and maybe she decided to go for a stroll."

"Nonsense," snapped Don Coyote, crawling out from under the bed and putting on his robe and his feather slippers. "I know a ghost when I see one!"

Eleanor Owl stepped into Don Coyote's room. "I could not help overhearing," she said. Eleanor Owl considered ghosts to be a very serious matter. She took out her pad and pencil. "Did the ghost say anything to you?"

"I didn't give it a chance," replied Don Coyote.
"But I *did* see it! And it has shortened my life!"

"There, there," said the hotelkeeper. "Try to get
some sleep."

Obviously Don Coyote was not up to answering
any further questions. Eleanor Owl and the hotelkeeper went back to their rooms, and Don Coyote
bolted his door. The hotel once again quieted down,
and soon all that could be heard was the occasional
lap of a wave on the beach.

8

Eleanor Owl and Mr. Paws were having a conference at breakfast.

"This certainly isn't the quiet, restful hotel Doctor Swan said it would be," said Mr. Paws. "Maybe we should move to Big Ruby's Hotel down the beach. I'm sure there aren't so many suspicious characters lurking about, or ghosts in the halls."

"We will do no such thing," said Eleanor Owl. "This hotel suits me just fine."

Mr. Paws could see that Eleanor Owl was enjoying herself.

"There *are* some strange goings-on here," said Eleanor Owl. "But mark my words, some even stranger things will occur. Something quite criminal, I should think. You know I have a nose for such things."

"Do you think Don Coyote really saw a ghost?" asked Mr. Paws.

"Certainly not," said Eleanor Owl. "But he saw something that *looked* like a ghost. And I mean to find out what it was."

9

By afternoon the hotelkeeper had a worried expression. The Cootie family had still not arrived.

"I hope they didn't change their minds, whoever they are," he said. "It's always nice to begin a summer with a full hotel."

Outside, MacTavish the postman stepped onto the wide verandah and wiped his perspiring brow. "What a hot day," he said, looking out at the glaring sun. "I'd much rather be taking a cool dip than lugging around this heavy pouch. This is really a job for a kangaroo. And my uniform is so itchy."

"Good afternoon, Hamish," said the hotelkeeper. "Anything for me?"

The hotelkeeper was always hopeful at mail time. And today perhaps there would be word from the Cooties.

"Not very impressive, I'm afraid," said MacTavish. "Only this wee package." And swinging the leather pouch off his back, he produced a small parcel wrapped in brown paper and tied with yellow yarn. It was addressed to the hotelkeeper.

"Hummm," said the hotelkeeper. "It's probably from my mother. She goes north for the summer, and she always sends me a souvenir."

"Aren't you going to open it?" asked MacTavish.

"In a moment," said the hotelkeeper. "May I interest you in a tall, cool glass of ice water?"

MacTavish accepted the ice water gratefully and sat

29

down in one of the comfortable wicker chairs on the verandah. "Do you have high hopes for the summer?" he asked the hotelkeeper.

"Oh my, yes," replied the hotelkeeper. "The hotel is already filled, with the exception of one family, the Cooties."

"Unusual name," said MacTavish.

"I'm quite worried," said the hotelkeeper. "They have never stayed here before, and I hope they didn't lose their way."

"Maybe they decided to stay at Big Ruby's Hotel down the beach," said the postman.

The hotelkeeper was truly shocked. "Hush your mouth!" he exclaimed.

"Sorry," said MacTavish.

While MacTavish crunched an ice cube, the hotelkeeper cut the yellow yarn with his penknife. Unwrapping the brown paper, he held up a tiny box, on which was written in a delicate hand, "Open with care."

"This is not from my mother," said the hotelkeeper.

Removing the lid of the box, he discovered two small envelopes, marked "One" and "Two."

"Who could this be from?" he said, tearing open the first envelope.

Inside was the following note:

Dear Hotelkeeper,

We are the Cootie family, husband and wife, son and daughter, and we have come for the summer. The children are well-behaved, and we have no pets. We shall require a large airy room with a view of the ocean. We apologize for the delay in arriving, but we had to stop off to visit relatives.

Yours sincerely,
Fred Cootie

P.S. We are in the envelope marked "Two."

The hotelkeeper opened, ever so carefully, the second envelope and peered inside. "Welcome to the hotel," he said.

10

"What's that?" cried Foster Pig, leaping out of bed and grabbing his flashlight. "What's that weird noise?" Foster cocked an ear and listened carefully. But the noise had suddenly stopped. "Sounded like someone moaning," said Foster, climbing back into bed and inserting his earplugs. "Perhaps it was only my imagination. Sensitive souls like myself often have very lively imaginations."

In their large room overlooking the water, the Cootie family huddled together. "Don't be afraid, children," said Fred Cootie, bravely. "It's probably just the night wind."

"This is a spooky place," said the Cootie kids.

In Room Thirteen, Don Coyote was hiding in the closet. "This is *it*," said Don Coyote, clutching his heart. "The old ticker is really going to stop this time." Don Coyote's paws were shaking. He felt that some of his fur might be falling out.

Eleanor Owl looked up from the detective story she was reading.

"What was that curious sound?" she asked herself. "This calls for a little investigating." Putting on her robe and fuzzy slippers, she stepped out into the hall.

"OOOOOH, EEEEEG, AHHHHHG, OOOOOH," something groaned.

But when Eleanor Owl moved in the direction of the sound, it suddenly stopped. "I can't be sure which room it was coming from," she said to herself. "But I have my suspicions."

Eleanor Owl stood in the hall for several minutes. She tried to be as quiet as possible. But the mysterious sound did not come again, and she went back to her room and her detective story.

"Wow!" exclaimed one of the squirrel twins to the other. "What a neat place!"

Miss Chicken, who was a very sound sleeper, was happily snoozing away and dreaming of all the wonderful things that had happened in her life. She did not hear the unusual and spooky sounds. She did not hear the doorknob to her room slowly turn.

11

A bright orange sun streamed through the open window. Birds sung in the trees, and a gentle breeze rustled the azalea bushes by the verandah.

The goose was the first to get out of bed in her room in the basement. After brushing her teeth and carefully folding her pajamas, she put on a fresh apron and hurried upstairs to the kitchen. Today she would try to make hot biscuits. Turning on the kitchen radio, she listened to the Ten Top Tunes of the day and did a little dance.

Upstairs, Foster Pig's snout soon began to twitch. "Hummm," he said. "I smell something that smells something like hot biscuits. I must hurry and take my morning constitutional before it's time for breakfast."

Others in the hotel began to stir.

Don Coyote came out of his closet and crawled into bed. "Maybe now I can get some sleep," he said, pulling the covers up over his head.

"It's going to be a beautiful day," said the hotelkeeper, looking out the window. "I must get myself organized." He checked his best hotelkeeper's smile

in the mirror. "A good hotelkeeper always starts the day with a smile" was one of his favorite mottoes.

Miss Chicken awoke refreshed from her uninterrupted sleep. "That's odd," she thought, looking around the room. "I could have sworn that I had tidied up before going to bed. So many of my things are out of place. I must be getting absent-minded. But why are drawers open? I *never* leave drawers open. And why is the top off of my hatbox?" Suddenly Miss Chicken realized the truth. "Someone has been in my room while I have been sleeping!"

Miss Chicken rushed to the lobby to inform the hotelkeeper.

"How unfortunate," said the hotelkeeper. "Nothing like this has *ever* happened at the hotel. I suppose there were things of great value taken?"

"No," said Miss Chicken, "nothing was taken. But someone *was* in the room."

"Hummm," said the hotelkeeper, scratching his beak. "A prowler. I shall look into this matter immediately."

12

"I don't want to alarm you," whispered the hotelkeeper to Eleanor Owl, "but there is a prowler in the
hotel. Someone has disarranged Miss Chicken's
room."

"I am not at all surprised," said Eleanor Owl.

"Will you assist me in this matter?" asked the hotelkeeper.

"Delighted," replied the detective, who felt herself
begin to tingle all over.

"Oh, I feel so relieved," said the hotelkeeper. "You
see, at hotelkeepers' school they did not teach us
what to do in a situation like this."

"Just leave it to me," said Eleanor Owl.

When the hotelkeeper had gone, Eleanor Owl
turned to Mr. Paws. "What did I tell you? *Criminal*
activity, just as I predicted."

"How shall we proceed?" asked Mr. Paws. He knew that Eleanor Owl was always very orderly in her investigating.

"First," said Eleanor Owl, "we must get our facts organized. "It is my suspicion that the entering of Miss Chicken's room and the other strange goings-on in this hotel are related."

"Someone is up to no good," said Mr. Paws.

"Exactly," said Eleanor Owl. "And it is not going to be easy finding out who. But I will find a way. Right now, I want to have a word with Miss Chicken. I'm curious to know why only *her* room was visited by The Prowler."

"I believe I saw her going out to the verandah," said Mr. Paws.

"Let the investigation begin," said Eleanor Owl.

13

"I could not help noticing that you are standing on your head," said Eleanor Owl.

"It is part of my yoga exercises," replied Miss Chicken, who was upside-down.

"Oh, I see," said Eleanor Owl. "Yoga is said to be excellent for the nerves. It makes one serene."

"Yes," said Miss Chicken. "The only way for me to remain calm is to do my yoga."

"How fascinating," said Eleanor Owl, who was always interested in learning something new. "May I try?"

"It's very easy," said Miss Chicken. "But you must begin very slowly."

Eleanor Owl took off her cloak and drew a deep breath. "What do I do first?"

Miss Chicken explained that standing on one's head required a lot of concentration. "First you must cup your head in your wings and bend slowly forward."

Eleanor Owl did as she was told. "I hope I don't fall over."

"If you do, you do," said the beautiful chicken. "It's all a question of getting your balance. Just like riding a bicycle."

Eleanor Owl bent ever so slowly forward, until her head was touching the floor.

"Now move your feet slowly toward your head. That's right," said Miss Chicken. "And now, with your stomach muscles draw your feet and legs into the air."

Eleanor Owl again did as she was told. "Am I doing this correctly?" she asked.

"You're almost there," said Miss Chicken. "Gently, gently. Now point your toes straight in the air. There, that's it!"

Eleanor Owl was very proud of herself. "This feels wonderful!" she exclaimed.

"That is the silliest thing I ever saw," snorted Foster Pig, stepping out onto the verandah.

"We are doing our yoga exercises," said Eleanor Owl. "Why don't you join us? Yoga is very good for the disposition."

"There is nothing wrong with my disposition, thank you," snapped Foster. "You won't catch me making a fool of myself."

Foster left the ladies to continue their yoga.

"Yoga would do that pig a world of good," said Miss Chicken. "He is always in a snit about something."

"Never mind him," said Eleanor Owl, still standing on her head. "I want to ask you a few questions."

"Go right ahead," said Miss Chicken.

14

Foster Pig stuck his snout in the air and sniffed the salty gulf breeze.

"There is nothing quite so pleasurable as a leisurely promenade before breakfast," said Foster, bending down to flick a few grains of sand from his handsome two-toned spats with his feather duster.

Lost in thought, Foster meandered down the beach. As far as the eye could see, there wasn't a soul, only an occasional merry sandpiper darting about on the clean white sand.

"Let's see now," said Foster, rubbing his chin. "First there was Horace Foster Pig, the founder of Foster Farms. Horace married Lavinia, who gave birth to Fenwick, Hyacinthe, Victoria, and James. James was my grandfather, and my grandmother was Hester, who gave birth to my father, Oliver. Oliver married Miranda. And then *I* was born — Foster Pig, of Foster Farms.''

Foster Pig enjoyed thinking about his family background. He loved the names of his ancestors, so important and distinguished-sounding. In fact, thinking about his family history was one of Foster's favorite activities.

Suddenly Foster stopped in his tracks! Out of nowhere the squirrel twins had appeared. They were laughing and racing each other to the water. Foster noticed it immediately — they weren't wearing their bathing trunks!

Foster was beside himself with rage! He waved his cane in the air! ''Outrageous! *Outrageous!*'' he cried, rushing after the squirrels.

''Make a run for it!'' cried one of the twins.

Foster Pig chased the squirrels down the beach. ''I'll teach you little demons!'' he cried. ''This isn't a zoo, you know! Bathing trunks are required at all times!''

When the angry pig paused to catch his breath, the squirrel twins scampered off into the dunes.

"Whoever heard of making such a fuss over a little furry dipping?" they said.

15

"Did you learn anything from Miss Chicken?" asked Mr. Paws.

"I'm not sure," said Eleanor Owl. "But I did learn how to stand on my head."

"What could The Prowler have been looking for?" asked Mr. Paws.

"If we knew that," said Eleanor Owl, "we would be on our way to solving this mystery."

"Tell me about Miss Chicken," said Mr. Paws.

"Oh, she has had a very interesting life," said Eleanor Owl. "Miss Chicken was once a famous circus chicken."

"That *must* have been exciting," said Paws. "Circus performers get to see so much of the world, all that traveling around."

"Yes, Miss Chicken has been all over the world," said Eleanor Owl. "She was a member of the famous Butterworth and Chang Circus, and she has been to Turkey, India, Japan, and Egypt."

"I have always wanted to visit Egypt," said Mr. Paws. "I would give anything to see a real mummy."

"Perhaps someday you will," said Eleanor Owl.

"Why did Miss Chicken leave the circus?" asked Mr. Paws.

"She decided that it was time to retire," said Eleanor Owl. "She felt she needed more time to be alone, to practice her yoga. The circus, you know, is very hectic, and Miss Chicken wanted a more simple life."

"That makes sense," said Mr. Paws.

16

"*Where* is my lunch?" demanded Foster Pig.

"I'm afraid there will be a slight delay," said the hotelkeeper. "The goose won't come out of the pantry. It seems she had another fright this morning."

"She's probably very high strung," said Don Coyote. "I can easily sympathize." He did not mention that he too was spending a lot of time in closets lately.

"There's nothing the matter with that goose," snapped Foster. "She's just slacking off. If there is anything I can't tolerate, it's someone who doesn't do his or her job properly. That goose should be replaced. The moment I laid eyes on her, I knew that the service here was going to be second-rate."

"What seems to have upset her?" asked Eleanor Owl, ignoring Foster Pig's irascible comments.

"All I know," said the hotelkeeper, "is that after breakfast she was busily making beds upstairs. Suddenly there was a terrific squawk, and she flew down the stairs. And now she has locked herself in the pantry."

"Which room was she in?" asked Eleanor Owl, taking out her pad and pencil.

"I believe she was in the Traveling String Quartet's room," answered the hotelkeeper.

"I see," said Eleanor Owl, raising an eyebrow. "And where were the ladies at the time?"

"They were in the dining room, lingering over their breakfast," said the hotelkeeper. "We were serving banana waffles."

Eleanor Owl whispered in Mr. Paws' ear. "In that case, the goose must have seen something."

"What do you suppose it could have been?" asked Mr. Paws.

"I have no idea," said Eleanor Owl, "but whatever it was, it must have been scary."

"Am I going to get my lunch or not?" shouted Foster Pig. "You know, this isn't the *only* hotel on the beach. I am told that the food at Big Ruby's is perfectly scrumptious."

"There, there," said the hotelkeeper. "I'll prepare lunch myself. How about a nice bowl of Cream of Junebug Soup?"

"Gag!" cried Foster Pig. "If there is one thing I can't stand, it's Cream of Junebug Soup!"

Mr. Paws looked out the dining room window. "Where do you suppose *they* are going?" he said.

"The baboon ladies seem to be taking that cello case for a walk," said Eleanor Owl.

"That's unusual," said Mr. Paws.

"It certainly is," said Eleanor Owl. "Everybody knows that sea air is not good for musical instruments."

"Perhaps," said Paws, his eyes brightening, "there is something other than a cello in that case!"

The four baboons wandered very far down the beach. Soon they had disappeared from sight.

17

Miss Chicken spread out her picnic blanket in a se-
cluded section of the dunes. Then she put on her
sunglasses and removed the contents of her basket
— one marmalade sandwich on white bread, a thermos of chocolate milk, and a slice of strawberry-
rhubarb pie.

"It's so nice to get away by oneself," thought Miss
Chicken, nibbling on her sandwich and sipping from
her thermos.

The sun was bright and hot, and after her snack
Miss Chicken lay on her back to tan her feathers. In
a moment she was sound asleep.

Suddenly Miss Chicken felt the presence of someone nearby. Her eyes fluttered open.

A sinister voice called out to her, "Your days are
numbered, Marietta Chicken!"

Miss Chicken sat up. Peering at her from the top of the nearest dune was a strange and ugly creature. It was wrapped from head to toe in old dingy bandages, and it had tiny mean-looking slits for eyes.

"Who are you?" asked Miss Chicken in a shaky voice.

"You know who I am and what I want," said the voice.

"Oh no I *don't!*" said Miss Chicken.

"Oh yes you *do!*" insisted the voice. "And if you don't give me what I've come for, you'll be really sorry! I'm giving you one last chance!"

All of a sudden, Miss Chicken found her courage. She flung a handful of sand at the creepy figure. "Get out of here, you big bully! I don't know what you're talking about!"

The figure retreated.

"Rats!" whispered a voice. "That chicken is tough!"

Hurriedly Miss Chicken gathered up her things and stuffed them into her picnic basket. Scratching up a great cloud of sand, she ran for the hotel.

18

Meanwhile Foster Pig was admiring himself in the long mirror on the closet door of his room.

"I look superb," he said, turning round and round.

Foster was wearing a colorful pair of silk bathing trunks, hand-painted with palm trees and dancing Hawaiian pigs in hula skirts.

"Absolutely superb," sighed Foster. "It's too bad there is no one here worth impressing, for I certainly have my share of charm and good looks."

Out on the beach some of the other guests were relaxing on the sand. The squirrel twins were busy building a large sandcastle with a moat and turrets. Eleanor Owl, Mr. Paws, and Don Coyote lay on beach blankets with their faces to the sun. The Coo·

ties, wearing tiny swimsuits and sunglasses, were sunbathing on a leaf.

The hotelkeeper gazed out at the beach from the verandah. "My guests certainly seem to be enjoying themselves. Maybe there will be no more unfortunate incidents."

"Oh, look!" whispered one of the squirrels. "Here comes Foster Pig. And he's wearing bathing trunks!"

"Doesn't he look ridiculous!" said his twin.

"Superb, superb," sang Foster to himself.

When Foster saw the two squirrels, he gave a disgusted snort and walked by without so much as a how-do-you-do.

The hotelkeeper called out to Foster, "Mr. Pig, the waves are very big this afternoon. It will be dangerous swimming."

"I'll have you know," said Foster Pig, "that I am an

excellent swimmer. No wave is too big for Foster Pig!"

"That pig certainly has a high opinion of himself," whispered Eleanor Owl to Don Coyote.

"Oh, look," said Don Coyote. "He's going into the water."

Foster Pig skipped merrily into the surf, waited for a large wave, and dove in. "I'll show them," he thought.

The enormous wave broke over Foster's head and knocked him head-over-heels. Saltwater went up his snout and into his ears. Seaweed clung to his stomach and feet.

"I seem to have miscalculated," thought Foster, trying to get his head above water.

Another wave, even larger, crashed over him. And still another. Finally, with all his might, Foster succeeded in righting himself.

"Are you all right?" cried out the hotelkeeper, who had rushed down to the beach.

"Don't worry about me," said Foster. "I can swim like a fish."

"You had better come in now," advised the hotelkeeper.

Suddenly a peculiar look came over Foster's face. "Oh my goodness," he said softly. "Something seems to have gone wrong."

Reaching down to pull up his bathing trunks, Foster realized that there was nothing to pull up! The last big wave had washed him completely out of his magnificent trunks. Turning red all over, Foster felt that nothing so humiliating had *ever* happened to him before!

"I wonder why Foster Pig isn't coming out of the water," said Mr. Paws.

By now, everyone on the beach was watching Foster Pig. Foster felt their curious stares and pretended to be observing the sea gulls gliding high above. The waves were a little smaller now, but they continued to bump him about. He dug his toes deeper into the sandy ocean floor and tried to remain upright.

"I don't deserve this," he said to himself.

Suddenly a horrible thought occurred to Foster. Very soon it would be low tide and the water would be receding! "Everyone will see," he thought.

The two squirrels stopped work on their sand castle. "What's that?" said one of them, pointing to a colorful piece of cloth that had washed up on the sand. On it were hand-painted palm trees and dancing Hawaiian pigs in hula skirts.

"Wow!" cried the other squirrel. "Foster Pig has lost his bathing trunks!" They jumped about with glee.

"Now who's not wearing bathing trunks?" they

called out to Foster. "This isn't a zoo, you know! Bathing trunks are required at all times!"

Foster Pig turned redder and redder. "I think I shall die of shame," he thought.

Now everyone on the beach was aware of the situation.

"Serves him right," said Eleanor Owl.

The squirrel twins continued to dance about. They tossed Foster's Hawaiian trunks back and forth. "Come out, come out!" they shouted to Foster.

"Perhaps I shall allow myself to be carried out to sea," thought Foster.

Suddenly Miss Chicken came tearing down the beach from the direction of the dunes. Her feathers were standing on end, her tongue was hanging out, and plastic spoons were falling out of her picnic basket. Rushing past the sunbathers, she dashed up the steps of the verandah and plopped down in a Bombay chair. "Whew!" she gasped, wiping her brow.

Eleanor Owl and Mr. Paws hurried to join Miss Chicken on the verandah. "Whatever is the matter?" asked Eleanor Owl.

Miss Chicken was completely out of breath. "I . . . have . . . had . . . such . . . a . . . fright," she managed to say between gasps and gulps.

"That seems to be happening quite a lot around here," said Eleanor Owl.

"Tell us all about it," said Mr. Paws.

Miss Chicken explained how a spooky creature with narrow slits for eyes had scared the wits out of her while she was sunbathing in the dunes. "If I didn't know better," said Miss Chicken, "I'd say the creature was a mummy."

"Now, now," said Eleanor Owl. "I'm sure there is a very simple explanation. It was probably just some kids from Big Ruby's Hotel acting up."

This suggestion seemed to calm Miss Chicken down. "Oh my, yes," she said. "I'm sure that's what it was. Of course. Just some kids acting up."

Foster Pig, taking advantage of everyone's interest in Miss Chicken, quickly emerged from the water and slipped on his trunks. "Whew!" he gasped.

"Look," said Mr. Paws. "Foster Pig has recovered his trunks. Maybe Foster will be a little less unpleasant from now on."

"I doubt it," said Eleanor Owl. "You can't teach an old pig new tricks."

19

Feeling much relieved, Miss Chicken went upstairs to change for dinner.

But on opening the door to her room, Miss Chicken immediately sensed that something was amiss. "Someone has been here again," she thought.

Closing the door behind her, she looked around. Everything *seemed* to be in place. No drawers were open, and her clothes were all neatly hung in her closet. Nothing was disturbed on the dressing table.

Finally Miss Chicken saw what was the matter. Written in her own lipstick across the mirror were the curious words:

SHEPSUTHEP HATSO SET MOTEF SNOOSET

HA SET SMUF KA KLUK

SNET SO IB TA SET NUK

HET HAP GRIT KUK!

(signed)
THE MUMMY
P.S. YOU KNOW WHAT THIS MEANS.
SO BEWARE!

Miss Chicken felt her throat begin to gurgle. "This is really scary," she thought. "And it is not the work of some kids acting up. I think I should report this to Eleanor Owl. *She* will know what to do."

Eleanor Owl was on the scene in a flash. She examined Miss Chicken's mirror. She walked about the room. She looked at Miss Chicken. She looked back at the mirror.

" 'Shepsuthep hatso set motef snooset ha set smuf ka kluk snet so ib ta set nuk het hap grit kuk!' " she read aloud. "Hummm," she said. "Most intriguing."

Mr. Paws entered the room. "What is that curious writing on the mirror?" he asked.

"It's perfectly simple," said Eleanor Owl. "Surely you recognize the famous Curse of King Kluk? 'Shepsuthep hatso set motef snooset ha set smuf ka kluk, snet so ib ta set nuk het hap grit kuk!' means in Egyp-

tian, 'Whoever disturbs the cozy slumber of the Great King Kluk, will be up to the neck in deep sand stuck.' ''

Miss Chicken felt herself becoming faint. She sat down.

"Golly," said Mr. Paws, reading the writing on the mirror. "It is signed 'The Mummy.' ''

"Exactly," said Eleanor Owl. "And if my suspicions are correct, the creature with the funny eyes that frightened Miss Chicken in the dunes this afternoon was the mummy of the Great King Kluk himself."

"Wow!" exclaimed Mr. Paws. "What is *he* doing in this hotel?"

"But everyone knows," said Miss Chicken, "that mummies are dead as doornails. And that creature spoke to me."

"It is quite clear that it was someone else's voice," said Eleanor Owl. "Someone brought the mummy of the Great King Kluk to this hotel to frighten you."

"Whoever it is is doing a good job of it," said Miss Chicken.

"Perhaps it is more than *one* person," said Mr. Paws, giving Eleanor Owl a look.

"Exactly," said Eleanor Owl. "It is now essential that we find out all we can about a certain foursome staying at this hotel."

"But how?" asked Mr. Paws.

"Somehow," said Eleanor Owl, "we must get inside their room and do some serious eavesdropping."

"That would be very sneaky," said Mr. Paws in a cautious voice.

"Merely good detective work," said Eleanor Owl. "Detectives are *supposed* to go sneaking about. That's how we find out things."

"Oh," said Mr. Paws. "But getting inside the baboon ladies' room without their knowledge is almost impossible."

"Nothing is impossible," said Eleanor Owl. "I'll think of something."

20

The next afternoon Mr. Paws joined Eleanor Owl for tea in her room. "Why are you smiling?" asked Mr. Paws.

"I believe," replied the great detective, "that I have found a solution to our problem. I have just sent for the Cooties."

"The Cooties?" said Paws.

At that moment a feathery knock was heard, and the goose entered carrying a small cream-colored envelope on a brass tray.

"Here they are now," said Eleanor Owl, taking the envelope from the goose. "That will be all, Maxine. Thank you very much, my dear."

The goose, humming a new tune she had just

heard on the radio, left the room and returned to the
kitchen.

Eleanor Owl delicately opened the envelope.
"Good afternoon," she said to the Cootie family.

"Thank you for inviting us to tea," said Fernanda
Cootie, fanning herself with a tiny feather.

"Ah, but you are invited for much more than tea,"
said Eleanor Owl. "How would you like to take part
in a daring and exciting adventure?"

"Oh goody," cried the Cooties. "We love excite-
ment. What's the adventure?"

While Mr. Paws poured tea into tiny teacups, Eleanor Owl explained. "As you may have noticed,

there have been some strange characters in this hotel."

"You mean that Traveling String Quartet," said Fred Cootie. "We have been wondering about them."

"And as you may have heard," continued Eleanor Owl, "there have been quite a lot of strange goings-on, even some criminal activity. It is my opinion that we should find out as much as possible about those baboons. Even if it means being a little sneaky about it."

The Cooties were fascinated. "Go on, go on," they said. They were all ears.

"Well," said Eleanor Owl, "that's where you come in."

"How can we assist you?" asked Fernanda.

"I think I understand," said her husband. "Eleanor Owl would like us to sneak inside the baboon ladies' room and do some spying."

"Exactly," said Eleanor Owl.

"It is my opinion," said Mr. Paws, "that it would be best to leave the two Cootie children behind. This adventure might prove too exciting for them."

"Aw," whined Ferdel and Fennimore Cootie.

"You'll do as you're told," said their mother.

"Now remember," said Mr. Paws to Mr. and Mrs. Cootie, "you must be very careful not to be seen. Those baboon ladies are very suspicious characters, and if they discover you, it could be curtains for the Cooties."

21

"I hope everything goes well for the Cooties," said Mr. Paws after dinner.

"So do I," said Eleanor Owl, who was relaxing in a Bombay chair and smoking an after-dinner pipe. "But we must do our part as well. It's important to distract the baboons long enough to give the Cooties time to slip into the room undetected."

"But the Cooties are so small," said Mr. Paws. "I'm sure the baboon ladies would never see them."

"No use taking unnecessary chances," said Eleanor Owl. Her voice lowered to a whisper. "Here comes the ladies now."

"Good evening, ladies," said Mr. Paws.

"Good evening," said the ladies. They seemed to be on their way to their room.

"Retiring so early?" asked Eleanor Owl.

"Yes," said one of the ladies. "We've had a busy day."

Eleanor Owl thought fast. "Oh my," she said. "Just when our friend Mr. Paws was about to favor us with a song."

Mr. Paws gave Eleanor Owl a quizzical look.

"And I'm sure," continued Eleanor Owl, "that you ladies, being musicians, would hate to miss him."

The ladies looked at one another. Mr. Paws looked at Eleanor Owl.

"We certainly would enjoy a tune or two," said one of the ladies.

And they all sat down.

Mr. Paws became very nervous. "But I don't know *how* to sing," he whispered to Eleanor Owl.

"Now, now," said Eleanor Owl in a loud voice. "Don't be modest. You have a *lovely* voice."

"But *what* will I sing?" said Paws.

"I have always been partial to 'The Owl and the Pussycat,'" said Eleanor Owl.

There was a look of panic on Mr. Paws' face. "I know the words, but I don't know the tune," he whispered.

"Then make something up," Eleanor Owl whispered back. "The ladies are growing restless."

Mr. Paws clasped his paws together, closed his eyes, pursed his lips, and cleared his throat. "This is going to be perfectly awful," he thought.

He began to sing. It was a version of "The Owl and the Pussycat" that *no* one had ever heard before. And it *was* perfectly awful. Eleanor Owl stuffed the tips of her wings in her mouth to keep from laughing out loud.

But the baboon ladies did not seem to notice anything unusual. Keeping time with the music, they swayed back and forth. They tapped their feet.

And when the song was over, they gave Mr. Paws a rousing round of applause.

"Perfectly lovely," said one of the ladies.

"Such grace and style," said another.

"Such talent," said the third lady.

"I've never heard anything like it," said the fourth lady.

And with that, the four ladies got up, thanked the singer again, and climbed the stairs to their room.

When they were out of earshot, Mr. Paws turned to Eleanor Owl. "Did you hear that?" he said proudly. "They said I was very good. Perhaps I should take up singing."

"I think you should stick to detective work," said Eleanor Owl.

22

The next morning, Mr. Paws rushed into the hotel dining room and quickly sat down.

"Good morning," said Eleanor Owl, who was having her breakfast. "My flapjacks are delicious."

Mr. Paws was very excited. "The Cooties have not returned to their room!" he exclaimed.

"Oh dear!" cried Eleanor Owl. "The Cooties have been captured! And it's all my fault! I should never have sent them on such a dangerous assignment! They weren't prepared, they had no experience! Oh, I shall never forgive myself!"

"Now, now," said Mr. Paws.

"We must act immediately," said Eleanor Owl. "We must rescue the Cooties at once!"

Mr. Paws followed Eleanor Owl out of the hotel dining room. In no time at all, he found himself in a scary place.

"I forgot to tell you that I am afraid of high places," he whispered.

"Try not to look down," answered Eleanor Owl. "And remember that we are doing this for the Cooties."

The famous detective and her assistant were standing side by side on the narrow ledge outside the baboon ladies' window.

"It's a long way down," whispered Paws.

"Hush," whispered Eleanor Owl. "I think they are leaving the room."

"We have just enough time for a lovely swim before lunch," said a voice.

"Let's hurry," said another voice.

Mr. Paws and Eleanor Owl heard the door slam and lock.

"Now *we* must hurry," said Eleanor Owl.

Quickly they pushed back the curtains and stepped through the window. Inside the air was stale and smelled of incense and old bananas. In a corner stood a cello case.

"I believe we know who's inside *that,*" said Eleanor Owl.

Mr. Paws shuddered. "But where are the Cooties?" he said.

"Let's look around," said Eleanor Owl. "And be careful where you step."

"I think I hear something," said Mr. Paws.

"Help, help!" cried two tiny voices.

"It's coming from that bowl," said Eleanor Owl.

Mr. Paws and Eleanor Owl looked into a bowl of sticky banana fudge that was sitting atop the chest of drawers.

"There they are," said Paws, squinting at the fudge.

"We fell in," said Fernanda Cootie. "It's so sticky, we couldn't get out. We are *so* ashamed."

Mr. Paws delicately extracted the Cooties from the bowl. "We were worried about you," he said.

"We're fine," said Fred Cootie. "And we have something to report. There is a *mummy* in that cello case!"

"Oh my!" said Eleanor Owl. "And what else do you have to report?"

"Not much else," said Fernanda. "I'm afraid we took a little nap when we fell in the bowl."

"Never mind," said Eleanor Owl. "The important thing is that you are safe."

"You had better leave quickly before the baboons return," said Mr. Paws to the Cooties.

"What about you?" said Fernanda Cootie.

"Don't worry about us," said Eleanor Owl. "Hurry along now."

Mr. Paws opened the door a fraction of an inch, and the Cooties slipped out into the hall. Mr. Paws closed the door behind them.

"What now?" he whispered. "Those ladies will be back from the beach any minute, and we don't want them to find us here."

"Oh yes we do," said Eleanor Owl. "Open that cello case."

"Me?" gulped Mr. Paws. "I couldn't."

"Oh, very well," said Eleanor Owl, who wasn't afraid of anything. "I'll do it myself."

Mr. Paws shut his eyes.

Unfastening the latches, Eleanor Owl pulled open the front of the case. "That's him, right enough," she said, peeking inside.

Mr. Paws opened one eye and peeked in too. "Wow!" he cried. "The Great Kluk himself. Isn't he creepy-looking?"

"That's the way mummies are supposed to look," said Eleanor Owl. "All mummies are creepy-looking. Help me lift him out."

"Me?" gasped Mr. Paws.

"Now, now," said Eleanor Owl. "I know what I am doing."

"Very well," said Mr. Paws, who did not like the idea at all.

Reaching inside the case, the great detective and her assistant took hold of the mummy and lifted him out of the case.

"He's very light," said Mr. Paws, trying not to look at the mummy's mean little eye slits.

"Quickly," said Eleanor Owl. "Help me put him under the bed."

"I don't understand," said Paws.

"You will," said Eleanor Owl.

The mummy of the Great King Kluk was carried across the room, laid gently on the floor, and pushed under the bed.

"There," said Mr. Paws. "What next?"

"Now *you* will get inside the case," said Eleanor Owl.

"Me?" groaned Mr. Paws.

"Exactly," said Eleanor Owl. "I'd do it myself, but I won't fit. Hurry now. We haven't much time. And listen carefully to my instructions."

23

A key turned in the lock.

"What a delightful swim," said one of the ladies, coming into the room. "So refreshing."

"It certainly was," said one of the other ladies. "Let's get out of these wet suits and into our clothes. Banana fritters are on the menu for lunch!"

Inside the closed cello case, Mr. Paws felt his heart pounding. "I hope I don't disappoint Eleanor Owl," he thought. "This is a very difficult assignment."

Outside on the ledge, Eleanor Owl stood perfectly still.

"Tomorrow we will try again," said the first lady. "We'll make that chicken crack if it is the last thing we do."

"Just a minute!" boomed a voice from inside the case.

The ladies stopped what they were doing and stared at the case.

"Did you hear what I heard?" said the first lady.

The other baboons were too frightened to reply.

"Now hear this!" announced the voice. "Are you listening?"

"We're listening, O Great Kluk," said the first lady.

All four baboons fell to their knees and bowed their heads to the floor.

Inside the case, Mr. Paws cleared his throat and tried to make his voice sound even deeper and angrier. "I am *most* displeased!" he called out.

"But Great Kluk," said the first lady, "why have you not spoken to us before?"

"I have been sleeping," said the voice. "For a long, long time."

"Tell us how we have displeased you," said the ladies.

"You have been behaving very badly," said the angry voice. "And you have quite a lot of explaining to do. First of all, I would like to know why you have been scaring a helpless chicken half out of her wits."

"We can explain everything," said the ladies.

"A wise idea," said the voice. "Start at the beginning."

"Well," said the first lady, "for several thousand years baboons have guarded the tomb of the Great Kluk in the Valley of the Nile."

"Of course," said the voice, pretending to know more than it did.

The lady continued. "It was the greatest honor to

serve at the tomb. Our ancestors and ourselves always made sure that things were neat and tidy and that no one disturbed the Great Kluk."

"Very thoughtful," said the voice.

"But then one day, not long ago," said the lady, "someone got inside the tomb and made off with all the treasure. Necklaces, rings, scarabs. Even the toys the Great Kluk had as a little tyke."

"Not my *toys!*" cried the voice.

"Everything," said the ladies, bowing their heads. "That thieving chicken took it all."

"But what makes you think it was Miss Chicken?" asked the voice.

"When we discovered the treasure was missing, we also found several feathers lying on the floor of the tomb," said the ladies. "A trail of feathers has led us to this very hotel. And it did not take us long to realize that Miss Chicken was the culprit. We heard her say herself that she has been to Egypt. And she has always behaved in a peculiar and suspicious way. She stands on her head a lot, and she is unusually serene. Chickens are not like that. *We* think that maybe she isn't really a chicken at all."

"May I come in?" said Eleanor Owl.

The baboons were surprised to see Eleanor Owl at their window. "Er, of course," they said.

Eleanor Owl stepped inside. "I could not help overhearing your interesting conversation," she said.

"We didn't want anyone to know our little secret until we recovered the treasure," said the baboons.

"So you disguised yourselves as traveling musicians," said Eleanor Owl.

"That is correct," said the baboons. "We don't know the first thing about music."

"And you brought along the mummy of the Great Kluk in hopes of frightening Miss Chicken into returning the treasure," said Eleanor Owl.

"That is correct," said the baboons. "But so far our plan has failed."

"For the simple reason," said Eleanor Owl, "that Miss Chicken is not the thief."

At this moment, Mr. Paws stepped out of the cello case. "It was getting very hot and stuffy in there," he said.

"You tricked us!" cried the baboons.

"Yes," said Eleanor Owl, "but now that we know why *you* have been acting so suspiciously, perhaps my assistant and I will be able to help you recover the treasure of the Great Kluk, who, by the way, is under the bed."

The baboons seemed confused. "But we were *sure* that Miss Chicken was the thief."

"You should leave the detective work to others," said Eleanor Owl.

"But the thief *is* in this hotel?" said one of the baboons.

"Oh yes," said Eleanor Owl. "Right under our noses."

24

After lunch Eleanor Owl and Mr. Paws strolled along the beach. A gentle afternoon breeze was rising and the sea was a deep green.

"Such a lovely place," said Eleanor Owl. "I'm so glad Doctor Swan recommended this hotel for our vacation, and I certainly want to return next year."

But Mr. Paws was thinking of other things. "Do *you* know who the thief is?" he asked.

"Not yet," said Eleanor Owl, "but I *do* feel that it is not Miss Chicken. A detective's intuition, I suppose. Besides, I like her."

"I remember that you were also very fond of Boris Mongoose," said Paws.

"I was wrong about Boris," said Eleanor Owl grumpily. She didn't like being reminded of her mistakes. "There are, however, quite a few other more likely suspects in this case."

"I can think of at least two," said Mr. Paws. "The important clue is feathers."

"You may be forgetting someone," said Eleanor Owl. "You don't have to be a bird to have feathers."

Mr. Paws thought for a moment. "I see what you mean," he said. "But how are we going to get the thief, whoever it turns out to be, to come out in the open?"

"We must use our imaginations," said Eleanor Owl. "Just as we tricked the baboons into admitting what *they* were up to, now we must play a trick on the thief."

"That will be hard," said Mr. Paws.

"I'll think of something," said Eleanor Owl.

Just then Don Coyote, sneezing into a tissue, passed them on the beach. "I know I should have gone to the mountains for my vacation," he muttered. "I think I am allergic to sand."

"I have an idea," whispered Eleanor Owl to Mr. Paws.

25

That same afternoon, someone in the hotel was writing another letter.

Dear Grandmother,

I have been doing what you told me — I have
been listening at keyholes.

The heat is on! Eleanor Owl knows all about
the treasure, and she knows that the thief is in this
hotel. But she does not know that *I* am the thief.

I must be even more careful now. If I play my
part right, no one will ever suspect me.

Don't worry. The treasure is in a safe place.

Love,
You·Know·Who

26

Eleanor Owl and Mr. Paws sat down at their favorite table for dinner.

"I am so hungry," said Mr. Paws.

Don Coyote, Foster Pig, Marietta Chicken, the squirrel twins, the baboon ladies, and the Cooties all came into the dining room.

"Outrageous," muttered Foster Pig. "The magnolias on my table are *not* fresh."

The hotelkeeper smiled at his guests and rubbed his wings together. "Tonight's specialty will be a delicious and appetizing stingray stew. The goose has spent all day in the kitchen preparing it."

"I can imagine," Foster Pig said.

The kitchen doors swung open, and the goose appeared carrying a large steaming bowl.

"And here it is *now*," said the hotelkeeper. "I'm sure that you will all find it to your taste."

"Smells awful," grumbled Foster. "But then, I'm not surprised."

"Oh goodness," said Don Coyote, "stingray stew always disagrees with me. I think I shall have some cottage cheese and peaches instead."

As the goose was dishing out the delicious stew, Eleanor Owl spoke to Mr. Paws in a voice louder than usual. "You know," she said, "whoever made off with the treasure of the Great Kluk is going to be sorely disappointed."

"Oh really?" said Mr. Paws, in a loud voice and looking around the room to make certain the conversation was being overheard.

"Yes," said Eleanor Owl. "I have just been reading the most interesting item in the newspaper. It seems that, according to scientists, once the Kluk Treasure has been removed from its sandy tomb it will begin to disintegrate in the open air."

"Oh really?" said Mr. Paws.

"Yes," said Eleanor Owl, "very soon the entire Kluk Treasure, even the toys the Great Kluk had as a little tyke, will turn to dust."

"But that is terrible," said Mr. Paws. "Can't anything be done to save the treasure?"

"I suppose not," said Eleanor Owl. "Thieves, you know, are often very stupid. Whoever took the treasure will probably not have sense enough to put it back in sand, the way it has been for thousands of years."

"Of course," said Mr. Paws.

Eleanor Owl and Mr. Paws continued their dinner.

"That stew wasn't very tasty," whispered Paws.

"Too watery," Eleanor Owl whispered back.

When it was time for dessert, the hotelkeeper began to look nervous. "I can't understand it," he said. "The goose is not in the kitchen. She seems to have stepped out."

"Probably ashamed of that disgusting stew," said Foster Pig. "Small wonder."

"I think I know where she is," said Eleanor Owl. "Follow me."

Eleanor Owl and Mr. Paws, followed by the hotel-keeper and all the other guests, hurried out to the beach.

"I could not help noticing, Maxine," said Eleanor Owl, "that you are buried up to your neck in sand."

"I got stuck," snapped the goose.

"Look!" cried out the baboons. "The goose is wearing the headdress of King Kluk!"

"Trying to bury the treasure, eh, Maxine?" said Eleanor Owl.

"I've been tricked!" snapped Maxine. "You'll pay for this, you old buzzard!"

"My, my," said Mr. Paws, "that doesn't sound like the sweet Maxine we all know."

"Shut your puss, puss," snapped Maxine.

"So it was Maxine!" cried the Cooties.

"I *knew* she wasn't a cook," said Foster Pig.

"Clam up, porker!" snapped Maxine.

"I'm calling the sheriff," said the hotelkeeper.

"You do that, turkey," snapped Maxine.

"How can we ever thank you?" said the baboons, turning to Eleanor Owl.

"My pleasure," said Eleanor Owl.

"Isn't it interesting," said Miss Chicken, "that the curse of King Kluk really came true?"

"Yes," said Mr. Paws, "Shepsuthep hatso set motef snooset ha set smuf ka kluk, snet so ib ta set nuk het hap grit kuk!"

"Knock it off!" snapped Maxine.

27

That afternoon, after Maxine was whisked off to jail, Eleanor Owl and Mr. Paws were relaxing on the verandah.

"Of course!" exclaimed Eleanor Owl suddenly. "How silly I was not to have been more observant. Do you realize that goose bears a striking resemblance to someone we knew several years ago?"

"Of course!" cried Paws. "The Mystery of the Whistling Grandmother!"

"Exactly," said Eleanor Owl. "Old Grannie herself. They put her away for a long long time. I imagine she is still in the clink."

"Like grandmother, like granddaughter," said Mr. Paws.

Out on the beach Miss Chicken was giving a yoga class to the other guests.

"Wow, this is fun," squeeled the squirrel twins.

"It certainly is," agreed the baboon ladies and the Cooties.

"Maybe it will help my sinus condition," said Don Coyote.

"I hope I don't fall over," thought Foster Pig.

The hotelkeeper appeared on the verandah beaming from ear to ear. "I'm so pleased," he said to Eleanor Owl and Mr. Paws. "I have finally outdone Big Ruby. I have just hired a real-live musical group to entertain my guests. It's a group called The Electric Nostrils."

"Sounds exciting," said Paws.

"And," said the hotelkeeper, holding up a letter that MacTavish the postman had just delivered. "I have just received a reservation from a new guest who will be arriving shortly. But whoever it is forgot to sign his or her name."

"Hummm," said Eleanor Owl, taking out her pad and pencil, "there's something suspicious about that."

"Now, now," said Mr. Paws. "Remember that we are still on vacation."

"Now, now, yourself," said Eleanor Owl.

MS READ-a-thon—
a simple way to start youngsters reading

Boys and girls between 6 and 14 can join the MS READ-a-thon and help find a cure for Multiple Sclerosis by reading books. And they get two rewards — the enjoyment of reading, and the great feeling that comes from helping others.

Parents and educators: For complete information call your local MS chapter. Or mail the coupon below.

Kids can help, too!